I'm Not An Alligator

SHERRY HASSON

PAGE PUBLISHING, INC.
Conneaut Lake, PA

First originally published by Page Publishing 2021

ISBN 978-1-64424-313-8 (pbk)
ISBN 978-1-6624-3438-9 (hc)
ISBN 978-1-64424-314-5 (digital)

Printed in the United States of America

Dedicated to Kimm, Bryan, Ender, Antonia, Levi, Corey, and the students of Southgate Academy, each one being uniquely different, yet find acceptance in one another and others.

This is Crocker.

Crocker is a crocodile, or so he's been told.

One day, when Crocker went down by the pond to swim, some of the bigger crocodiles began to tease him.

"Crocker is a gator, a gator, a gator," sang those mean old crocs. "Crocker is a gator, and he can't play with us!"

"You can't swim with us, Crocker. You're an alligator, and today, only crocodiles are allowed in the pond," they teased with an awful laugh.

"I am a crocodile. I am, I am," shouted Crocker.

He was so mad that he lowered his brows, gritted his teeth, and took off running home. He ran as fast as his little legs would go, and when he was far enough away from the pond, he let out a big, big scream.

"Those are the meanest crocs I've ever seen," he screamed. "They are bullies! Bullies they are!"

Crocker was troubled for days and days. Back and forth he would go to the mirror, back and forth, back and forth. "I don't look like an alligator, or do I?" he thought. "Do I really look different than those crocs by the pond?"

"I'm a crocodile. I am, I am," he said, looking one last time in the mirror.

Crocker didn't like being called an alligator.

Then Crocker thought about his friends, Al and Allie. They were alligators. They would know if he was a crocodile or not. He would go down by the swamp and ask them.

It didn't take long for Crocker to find Allie. She was on the path that led to the swamp.

As soon as their eyes met, Allie could tell Crocker wasn't at all happy. Not at all!

"What's wrong, Crocker?" she said. "You look sad."

"Hi, Allie," said Crocker. "I am sad. The crocs down by the pond would not play with me because I was not like them."

"Those crocs are bullies," said Allie. "They were not being nice when they wouldn't let you swim in the pond. Let's go play by the swamp."

Seeing that Crocker was still not happy, Allie asked, "What else is making you sad, Crocker? Do you want to talk about it?"

With a big moan and lots of crocodile tears, Crocker cried out, "Those mean old crocs said I wasn't a crocodile. Do I look like you?"

"Yes, you do," said Allie. Alligators have sharp teeth and very long tails. You and I have sharp teeth and very long tails too."

"But I'm not an alligator," cried Crocker. "I'm a crocodile. I am, I am."

"Well, you look like an alligator to me," said Allie giving Crocker a hug. "However, crocodiles have sharp teeth and very long tails too. Let's go ask Al. I think he is swimming in the swamp. Maybe he will know."

Off to the swamp they went. As they walked, Crocker told Allie how the old crocodiles had teased him and how bad it made him feel.

"That was mean," said Allie. "I'm sorry you got your feelings hurt, but it doesn't matter what you are, Crocker. You are still my friend."

As they reached the edge of the swamp, they could see Al walking out of the muddy water.

"Hello, Al," said Crocker. "Do I look like you?"

"Of course you do," said Al. "We are alligators. We have sharp teeth, long tails, and short legs."

Just then, Crocker let out a great big wail. It was an awful sad wail! "I'm not an alligator," he cried. "I'm a crocodile. I am, I am!"

Al gave Crocker a hug. "I am sorry, Crocker, but you look like an alligator to me," said Al. "However, crocodiles also have sharp teeth, long tails, and short legs. It doesn't matter what you are, Crocker. You are still my friend. We can ask Snapper. He may know what you are. He's down by the Cattail Bridge."

"I don't know Snapper," said Crocker rubbing the tears from his eyes. "And I don't know if he will be my friend, or if he will be mean to me like those other crocs were."

"Snapper is nice, and he is kind," said Allie. "You will like him, Crocker.

Making new friends can be scary, but it can be fun too. Speaking of fun, let's race to the swamp!"

Al and Allie looked at each other with a grin. Crocker's frown had turned upside down! "One, two, three, let's go," shouted Crocker with a smile.

"Hi, Snapper," said Al." This is Crocker. Does he look like you?"

"Of course he does," said Snapper. "We're alligators. We have sharp teeth and long tails. We also have short legs and webbed feet. Yes, he's an alligator all right."

"But I'm not an alligator," Crocker said with those big crocodile tears in his eyes. "I'm a crocodile. I am, I am!"

"Cheer up, Crocker," said Snapper. Maybe you are a crocodile. They have sharp teeth, long tails, short legs, and webbed feet too. However, it doesn't matter what you are. You are still my new friend. This might cheer you up. It's a hat like mine. I give one to all my new friends. We can be twins. Now let's go play!"

Crocker didn't want to be twins. Snapper was an alligator. Crocker did not want to play. He couldn't. He could not! He wouldn't. He would not! Not until he knew what he was. So the three little friends spent the rest of the afternoon trying to make Crocker feel better, but nothing seemed to help, not even his new baseball cap.

Al and Snapper began to think of who might be able to help Crocker with his question. They thought, and they thought. Then Al had an idea.

"Hey, Crocker," said Al. "Do you know old Mr. Sharptooth? He is very wise, and he is a crocodile. He will know what you are. Let's ask him."

"That's a great idea," said Snapper. "Come on, Crocker! The sun is going down, and we must go soon. Let's go!"

Passing by the everglades, where the old crocs hang out, they saw Mr. Sharptooth talking with Mr. Snapdragon.

"Mr. Sharptooth," they yelled. "Come here, come here!"

Crocker was so excited that his new hat blew off as he ran. All he could think about was asking the wise old croc the question. After all, he was a crocodile.

Faster and faster, he ran. He ran faster than Snapper. He ran past Al. Then he ran past Allie who was faster than fast!

"I know Mr. Sharptooth will tell me! He's a crocodile. He will know," shouted Crocker. "I am sure he will know!"

As he got closer to the old croc, he began to shout, "Mr. Sharptooth, Mr. Sharptooth!"

Mr. Sharptooth and Mr. Snapdragon could tell that Crocker had been crying. There were no great big crocodile tears left, but his eyes were redder than red.

"Crocker, are you all right?" said Mr. Sharptooth.

"No, I am not all right," said Crocker, bursting into tears. "Mr. Sharptooth, I know you are very wise, and I want to know what I am. Some of the other crocs wouldn't let me swim in the pond. They said I was an alligator, not a crocodile, so they wouldn't let me play. Do you know what I am?"

Mr. Sharptooth smiled. "Of course, I do. Alligators and crocodiles are from the same family. Look at Mr. Snapdragon and I. We may look the same because of our sharp teeth and bumpy backs. That's because we are Crocodilia. Our webbed feet and long tails look the same too."

Crocker didn't know if he was ever going to find out! If alligators and crocodiles looked the same, how would he know if he was a crocodile? Then Mr. Sharptooth said something that Crocker could see.

"Look at Al and Allie. Now look at me," said the wise old croc. "Can you see that you and I are lighter than Al and Allie? Now, look at Snapper's nose. He has a U-shaped nose, and ours is V-shaped."

"Of course I know what you are," said Mr. Sharptooth. "You're a crocodile, Crocker!"

"I knew it!" said Crocker jumping up and down.
''I am a crocodile. I am, I am."

That made Crocker very happy. Now he was ready to play with his friends.

THE END

About the Author

Sherry D. Hasson currently lives in Tucson, Arizona. As an Irish American, separated from her siblings since early childhood, she is no stranger to the emotional challenges children battle in finding acceptance. Sherry has dedicated her life to helping others learn and become happy with who they are and to be proud of their heritage. As the founder of SGA Charter School and the MACILOS program (Making A Change in Lives of Students), she has spent the last 23 years bringing people together from all walks of life, to create a legacy of love, care, and compassion for others. It is hoped that the reader will be inspired to find their inner strength to overcome obstacles in their lives, learn the importance of loving oneself and the value of true friendship.

CPSIA information can be obtained
at www.ICGtesting.com
Printed in the USA
BVHW021257290321
603649BV00003B/15